SARA FANELLI

MY MAP

BOOK

ABC
London

CASTLE
BRIDGE
TREASURE
MAP
KNIGHTS
SERVICES ✣ FOR KING
RIVER
!!!
N
W
E
S
my treasures

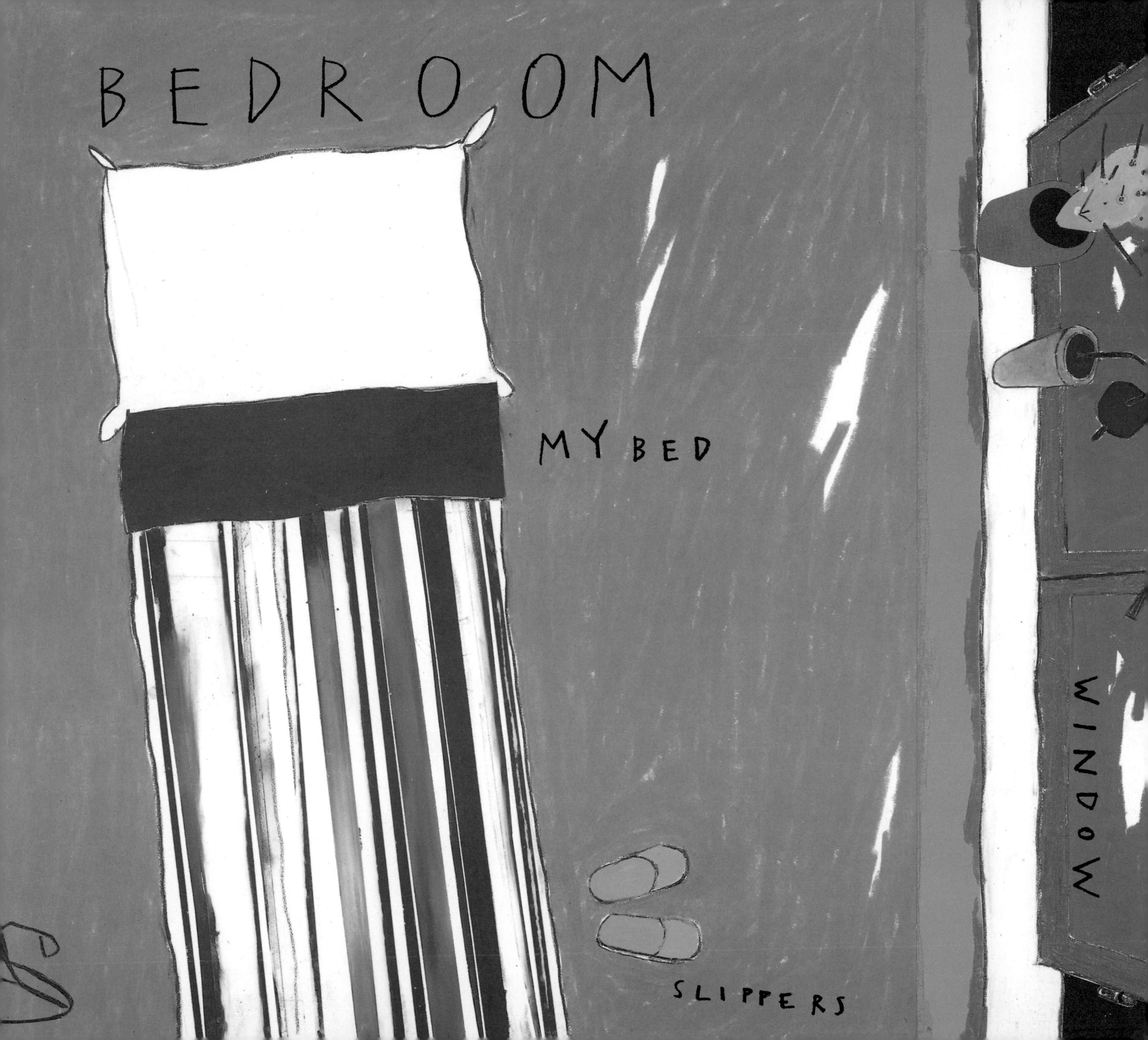
BEDROOM
MY BED
SLIPPERS
WINDOW

MAP
OF MY
FAMILY

ME

MUMMY

+ MY DOG
BUBU

GRANDPA
+
GRANDMA

MY SISTER

DADDY

COUSIN LOUISE

COUSIN PETER

COUSIN GEORGE

AUNT LUCY

UNCLE MICHAEL

AUNT ROSE

GRANDMA
+
GRANDPA

MAP OF MY DAY
MORNING
BREAKFAST
MILK
saturdays + sundays (NO school!)
schoolbus
SCHOOL

LUNCH

PLAYGROUND

my favourite games

HOME

SUPPER

STORY TIME

SPAGHETTI
↙

CAKES

KNIFE
↙
↓

↓

FORK
↓

↓

MILK

FOR GOOD
TEETH

↓ my favourite foods

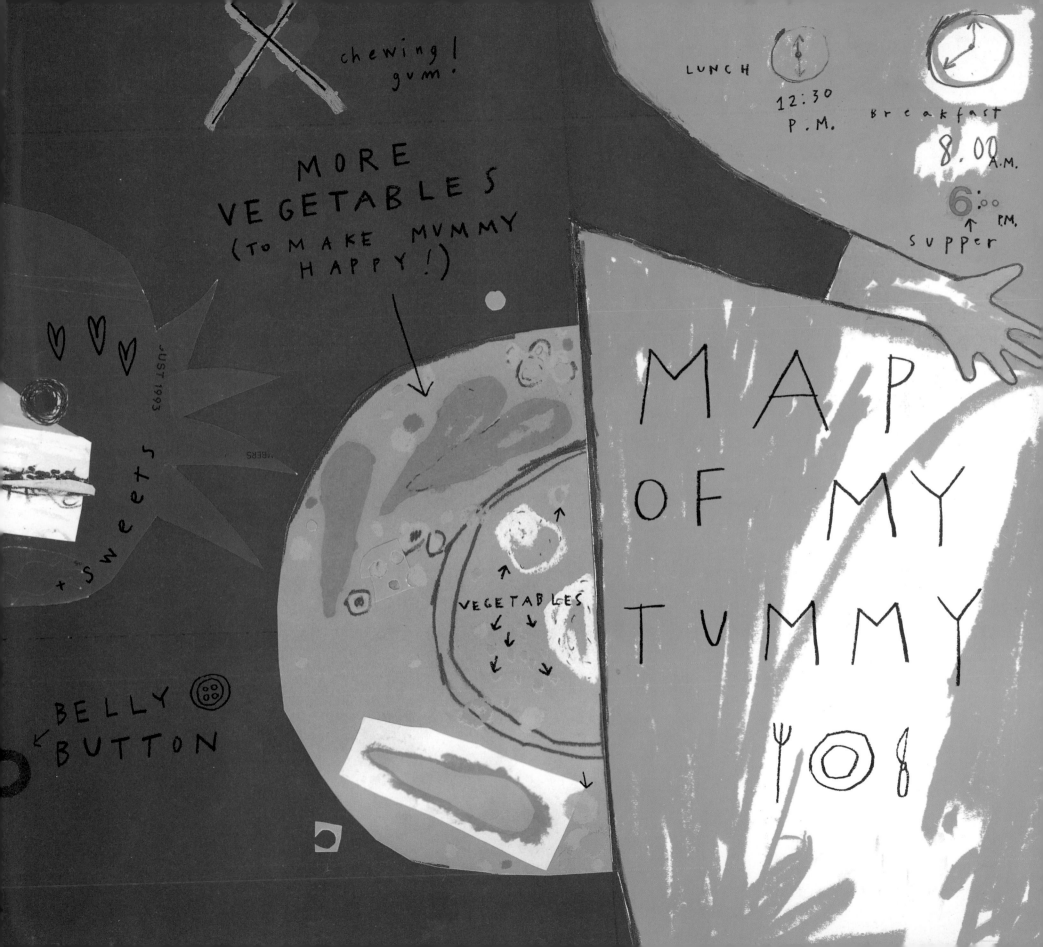

green

FROG

GREEN

BLUE

COLOUR

my favourite colour

YELLOW

BROWN

= BLUE +
RED +
YELLOW

BRIGHT
YELLOW
SUNSHINE

ORANGE

BLUE SKY

VIOLET

BLACK

WHITE

RED

GREY

THE COLOUR
OF CHERRIES!

MAP

RED +
WHITE =

PINK

(LIKE
THE
SKY
ON
A
RAINY
DAY)

FRIENDS

MOON + STARS ALBERTINA MY

SISTER

BOOKS

MAP OF MY HEART

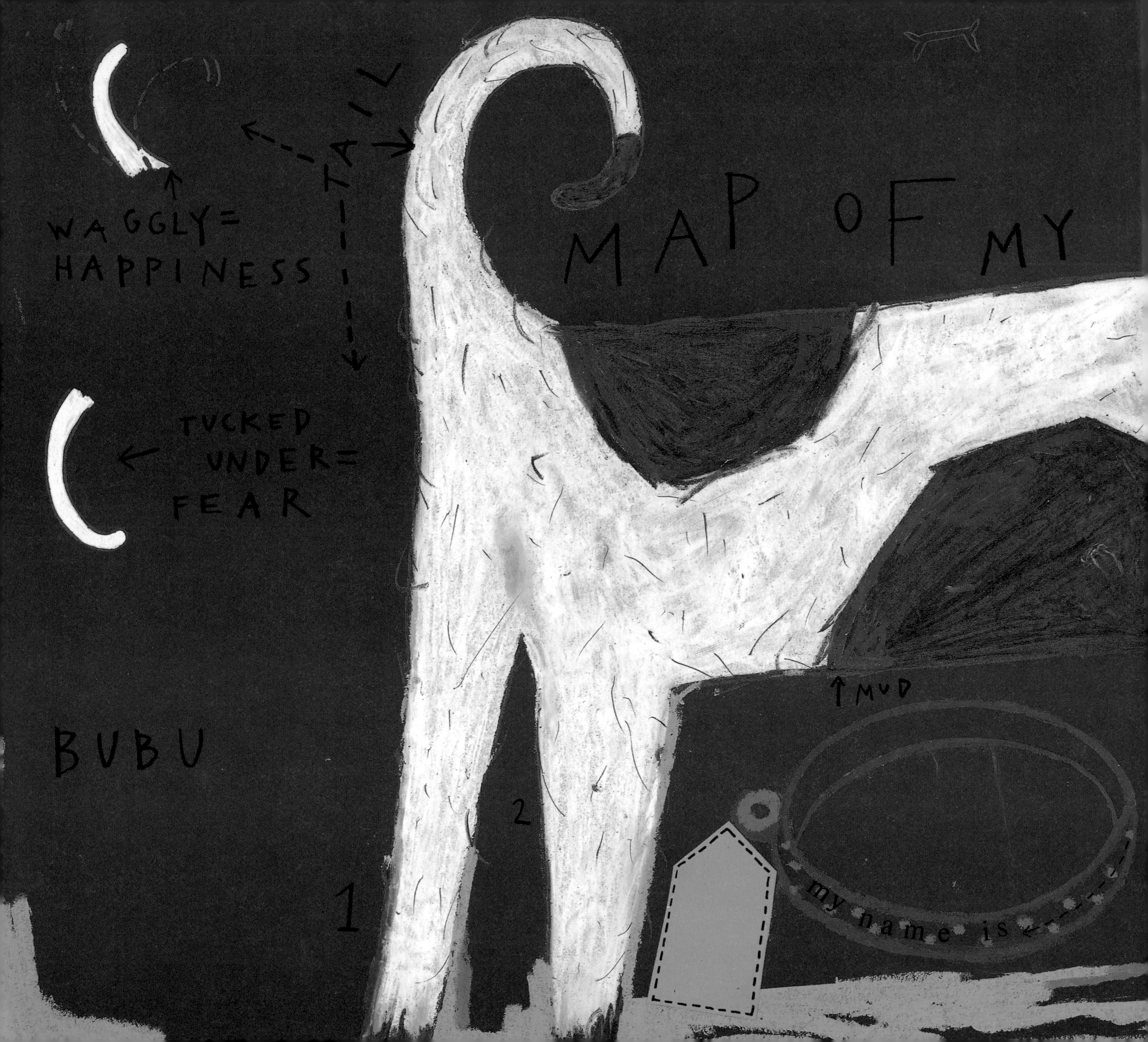
MAP OF MY
TAIL
WAGGLY=
HAPPINESS
TUCKED
UNDER=
FEAR
BUBU
MUD
2
1
my name is

DOG
DOG'S DREAM
POINTED EARS = ALERT
3
MUD →
4 LEGS
WET NOSE = HEALTHY DOG

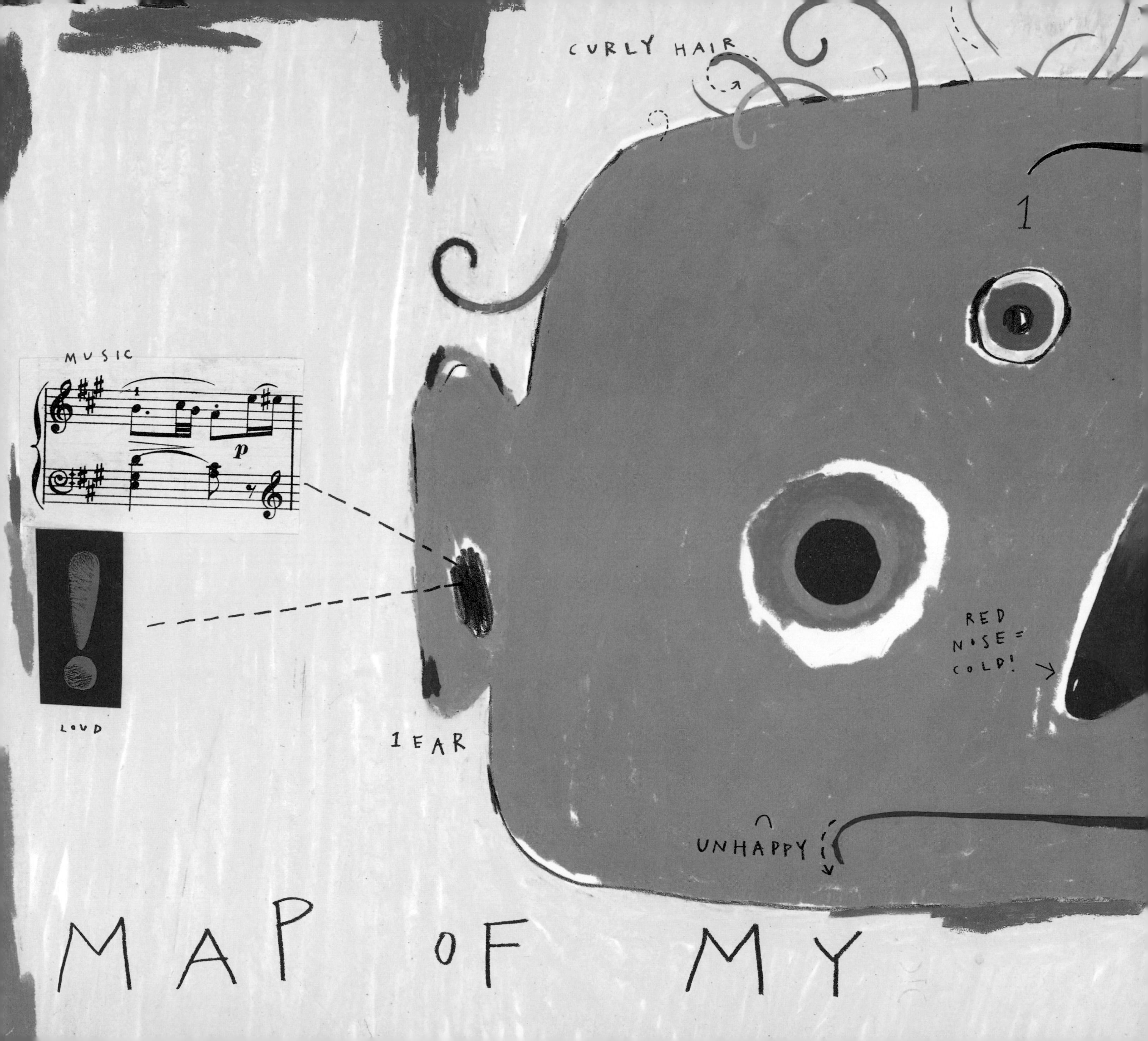
CURLY HAIR
1
MUSIC
LOUD
1 EAR
RED NOSE = COLD!
UNHAPPY
MAP OF MY

ICE-CREAM VAN
BEACH UMBRELLA
CHOCOLATE
PISTACHIO
DECK CHAIRS
LIFEGUARD
CABINS
SAND CASTLE
BUBU
MAP

BUOY ↑

BOAT ↗

A SCHOOL
OF 6 FISH

SAILBOAT

OF THE SEASIDE

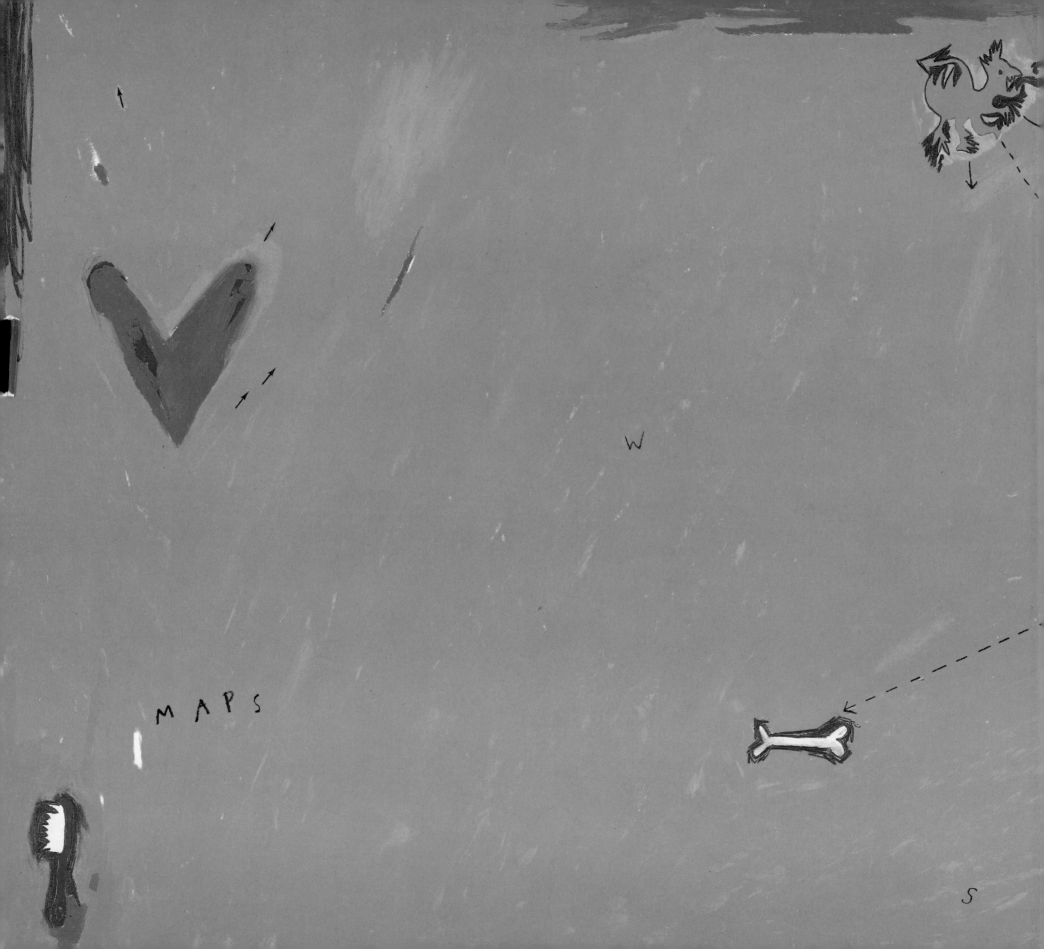